P9-CWD-858

Merry Christmas
Sarah,

Come
visit me in Boston!

Love from,
Aunt Jenny
December 1995

I HAVE AN AUNT

by Kathryn Lasky

illustrated by Susan Guevara

ON MARLBOROUGH STREET

Macmillan Publishing Company   New York

Maxwell Macmillan Canada   Toronto

Maxwell Macmillan International   New York   Oxford   Singapore   Sydney

Text copyright © 1992 by Kathryn Lasky
Illustrations copyright © 1992 by Susan Guevara

All rights reserved. No part of this book may be reproduced or transmitted in any form or by any means, electronic or mechanical, including photocopying, recording, or by any information storage and retrieval system, without permission in writing from the Publisher.

Macmillan Publishing Company is part of the Maxwell Communication Group of Companies.

Macmillan Publishing Company
866 Third Avenue
New York, NY 10022

Maxwell Macmillan Canada, Inc.
1200 Eglinton Avenue East
Suite 200
Don Mills, Ontario M3C 3N1

First edition
Printed in the United States of America

1 3 5 7 9 10 8 6 4 2

The text of this book is set in 15 pt. Esprit Book.
The illustrations are rendered in watercolors.

Library of Congress Cataloging-in-Publication Data
Lasky, Kathryn.
I have an aunt on Marlborough Street / by Kathryn Lasky ;
illustrated by Susan Guevara.
p.   cm.
Summary: Phoebe describes her many visits during the year to her Aunt Phoebe, who lives in
an old part of Boston where the sidewalks are made of brick and the houses touch shoulders.
ISBN 0-02-751701-2
[1. Boston (Mass.)—Fiction.   2. Aunts—Fiction.]   I. Guevara, Susan, ill.   II. Title.
PZ7.L3274Iac   1992   [E]—dc20   91-279

To my mother, Joyce,
and my great-grandmother, Fay

—S.G.

I have an aunt on Marlborough Street. She lives in a brick building on a brick sidewalk. Her name is Phoebe and so is mine. My mother takes me on the train to my Aunt Phoebe's.

The trip is only a half an hour, but it feels as if I have traveled half the world away from cement sidewalks and lawns and shopping malls to a part of Boston where some of the sidewalks are still made of brick and lots of the streetlights are lit with gas. And the chimneys have pots that look like funny hats: some like top hats, some like knights' helmets, some like peaked clowns' hats. The pots keep out the rain.

All of the buildings touch shoulders on Marlborough Street. There are no side yards, just little front yards no bigger than bedrooms. Aunt Phoebe's yard is filled with ivy. It has a fence around it that looks like black embroidery, but is really made of iron. In the middle of the yard there is one tree—a magnolia.

Almost every house on Marlborough Street has one magnolia tree and they bloom in the earliest spring. Their blossoms are nearly white and just barely pink. And by the second week in April the street looks like it's snowing magnolias.

Most of the buildings are made of brick. Some are orangy brick, some are deep red, some are dusty red. But there are three in a row made of white stone. Aunt Phoebe and I call them The Brides. There is one dark stone building across the street at number 14A. She is gray with black shutters and stands as straight as a pilgrim. So we call her the Pilgrim Lady. We say that she only dresses up twice a year—in April when the magnolia tree blooms, and in December when she wears her Christmas lights and green wreath.

When I come in the spring I help Aunt Phoebe plant the giant stone vases on the front steps of the building. Aunt Phoebe lets me pick out the plants at the flower shop around the corner. "You dare with color!" she said one day when I picked out some bright blue pansies and then chose orange marigolds.

Aunt Phoebe doesn't have fancy gardening tools. So we just use old forks and big kitchen spoons to loosen the soil and dig the holes. And one year when the hose was broken we had to use an old chipped china teapot to water the plants.

Every spring after we plant the vases Mrs. Martesi, who lives on the first floor, writes us a note: "Dear Phoebes— Thank you for the lovely flowers. They brighten my day." Mrs. Martesi is very old and very shy. I used to think only children were shy until I met Mrs. Martesi. I see her peeking out at the flowers from behind her curtains and watching the people in the street. But sometimes she will open her door just a crack and peep out and crook her finger toward Aunt Phoebe and me. "Phoebes!" she calls. Her voice always sounds a little creaky as if she doesn't use it very much. But I get excited because it means that she has been baking. She always hands me a box. It is usually a tin one with a fancy design of flowers or old-fashioned ladies in beautiful dresses. Taking off the lid is like looking into a jewelry box. There are little cakes with glistening frosting and pictures painted in colored sugar—butterflies and ballerinas, ladybugs and flower baskets. Aunt Phoebe says that Mrs. Martesi is not just a good baker, she is an artist.

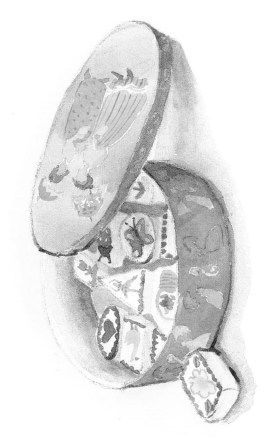

Inside Aunt Phoebe's apartment there is nothing really brand new, and some of the ordinary things seem either a little bit smaller or a little big bigger than usual. The refrigerator is very small but the bathtub is huge and has monster's feet with claws. Aunt Phoebe paints the toenails on each claw with her brightest nail polish. We often do our nails, Aunt Phoebe and me: fingers and toes, and she lets me touch up the tub's if they are chipped.

In the living room she has four lamps with regular lampshades, but the fifth light—the one over the dining room table—has an old-fashioned lace petticoat for a shade. It makes the light as soft as the moon in a blizzard.

We eat Chinese food from Lum Gardens at the table under the petticoat lamp and read our fortune cookies.

"You have the chance of becoming a great movie star!" Aunt Phoebe's fortune cookie says. Mine is not nearly so good. "Work hard and your efforts shall be rewarded."

We have a deal, Aunt Phoebe and me. If one of us gets a bad fortune she gets to be a part of the other person's good fortune. So Aunt Phoebe says.

"I can see it now: a movie starring The Two Phoebes. Our name in lights." I laugh and think about it. Double Phoebes in lights.

After dinner we used to play tiddlywinks, but the little disks kept getting lost in the cracks between the old floorboards. So now we play cards.

We stay up in our nightgowns until almost midnight. We eat our cakes, the ones Mrs. Martesi gave us, very slowly. I choose one with a butterfly and leave the wings for last.

There is only one bedroom and one bed at Aunt Phoebe's, so I sleep on the couch in the living room. We put a sheet on the couch and tuck it in under the cushions, and then another sheet on top. And then on top of that sheet there is an old patchwork quilt with designs of birds and hearts and flowers and stars and rabbits. My great grandma made it. She was the first Phoebe. Aunt Phoebe is the second Phoebe and I am the third Phoebe. So when she tucks me in and kisses me good-night she always says.

"Good-night.
Sleep tight.
Don't let the bedbugs bite.
Three Phoebes in the night!"

I can touch my great grandma's initials stitched in the corner. I keep that corner near my face and I watch the moon float over the rooftops and see the chimney pots become shadowy hats against the night. Sometimes, when the moon shoots its silver light into the living room through the petticoat lampshade, the walls around me turn to lace.